YASMIN

The Superhero

written by
SAADIA FARUQI

illustrated by
HATEM ALY

PICTURE WINDOW BOOKS
a capstone imprint

To Mariam for inspiring me, and Mubashir for helping me find the right words—S.F.

To my sister, Eman, and her amazing girls, Jana and Kenzi—H.A.

Yasmin is published by Picture Window Books, a Capstone imprint
1710 Roe Crest Drive
North Mankato, Minnesota 56003
www.mycapstone.com

Text © 2019 Saadia Faruqi
Illustrations © 2019 Picture Window Books

Library of Congress Cataloging-in-Publication Data
Names: Faruqi, Saadia, author. | Aly, Hatem, illustrator.
Title: Yasmin the superhero / by Saadia Faruqi ; illustrated by Hatem Aly.
Description: North Mankato, Minnesota : Picture Window Books, [2019] | Series: Yasmin | Summary: Yasmin gathers a cape and mask and sets out to find a villain to defeat with her "super powers"—however there are no villains hiding on her block, just neighbors who need a little help.
Identifiers: LCCN 2018046795| ISBN 9781515837831 (hardcover) | ISBN 9781515845799 (paperback) | ISBN 9781515837886 (eBook PDF)
Subjects: LCSH: Muslim girls—Juvenile fiction. | Pakistani Americans—Juvenile fiction. | Superheroes—Juvenile fiction. | Helping behavior—Juvenile fiction. | Neighbors—Juvenile fiction. | CYAC: Muslims—Fiction. | Pakistani Americans—Fiction. | Superheroes—Fiction. | Helpfulness—Fiction. | Neighbors—Fiction.
Classification: LCC PZ7.1.F373 Yk 2019 | DDC [E]—dc23
LC record available at https://lccn.loc.gov/2018046795

Editor: Kristen Mohn
Designer: Lori Bye

Design Elements:
Shutterstock: Art and Fashion, rangsan paidaen

TABLE OF CONTENTS

CHAPTER 1

Super Yasmin

Yasmin loved reading with Baba. Her favorite stories were about superheroes.

Baba closed the book.

"I wish I were a superhero," Yasmin said.

"What do you like about superheroes?" Baba asked.

Yasmin thought. "Well, they save people," she said.

"From what?" asked Mama.

"From evil villains, of course!"
Yasmin said.

Mama laughed. "Enough
reading," she said. "The weather
is perfect. Why don't you go
outside and play?"

Yasmin skipped to Nana and Nani's room. "I'm Super Yasmin!" she announced. "I'm going outside to defeat evil villains!"

"That sounds like important work," Nani said. "But every superhero needs a costume."

Nani took her dupatta and draped it over Yasmin's shoulders. "Here is your cape."

Nana brought out his old sleep mask. He cut two holes for Yasmin's eyes.

"Now you look just like a

superhero," Nana said.

"Thanks!" Yasmin waved.

"I'm off to save the world!"

CHAPTER 2

Who Needs Help?

Yasmin went outside. Lots of children were playing. Some rode bikes. Some kicked a soccer ball.

Yasmin searched everywhere. She didn't see any evil villains. What was the point of being a superhero if there were no villains to defeat?

"Hello, Yasmin!" It was

Emma's mom. She was bringing

in groceries from her car. Oops!

A bag fell and groceries rolled

down the street.

Yasmin ran and caught them all. "Here you go, Mrs. Winters," she said.

"Oh, you saved the day, Yasmin!" Mrs. Winters said. "Thank you so much."

Yasmin continued

her search for

villains. Maybe one

was hiding behind

this tree! Nope.

"Hey, Yasmin," Ali

called from his front porch. "This

math problem is really hard.

Can you help me?"

Yasmin figured out the

answer in a jiffy. "Four hundred

and seventy-five," she told him.

"You're so good at math, Yasmin," Ali said. "Thanks a million!"

Yasmin waved and kept walking. She needed to find a villain.

CHAPTER 3

A Real Hero

At the end of the street, a little girl was crying. Her ball was stuck on a roof. Yasmin looked around. A big stick lay on the ground.

"Don't worry," she told the little girl. "This will do the trick."

The girl was happy to get her ball back. "Thank you! Thank you!" She jumped up and down.

"You're welcome," said Yasmin.

Where were all the villains? she wondered.

Yasmin went back home,
disappointed. Baba was waiting
for her with a glass of cool lassi.

"Super Yasmin is back!"
Baba said.

"I'm not a superhero," Yasmin mumbled. "I didn't find a single evil villain to defeat." She took a sip of her lassi and sighed.

Baba hugged her close. "I saw that you helped many people on our street today," he said. "That's what real superheroes do!"

"They do?" asked Yasmin.

"Of course! Evil villains are only in story books," Baba said. "In real life, superheroes are the ones who go out of their way to be kind and helpful."

Yasmin gulped down her lassi. "You're right. I did help!" she exclaimed. "I guess I really am Super Yasmin!"

Baba laughed. "Come inside now," he said. "Even superheroes have to do their homework."

Think About It, Talk About It

❋ Superheroes have special powers or abilities—and so do people! What do you think Yasmin's super powers are? What are your super powers?

❋ Make up a superhero of your own. Draw a picture and give him or her a name. What special skills does your superhero have? Is there a particular problem your superhero must solve?

❋ Think about someone you admire, someone who is super! What do you admire about this person? What special skill do they have that makes them a superhero?

Learn Urdu with Yasmin!

Yasmin's family speaks both English and Urdu. Urdu is a language from Pakistan. Maybe you already know some Urdu words!

baba (BAH-bah)—father

dupatta (doo-PAH-tah)—a shawl or scarf

jaan (jahn)—life; a sweet nickname for a loved one

kameez (kuh-MEEZ)—a long tunic or shirt

lassi (LAH-see)—a yogurt drink

nana (NAH-nah)—grandfather on mother's side

nani (NAH-nee)—grandmother on mother's side

salaam (sah-LAHM)—hello

shalwar (SHAL-wahr)—loose pants

shukriya (shuh-KREE-yuh)—thank you

Pakistan Fun Facts

Yasmin and her family are proud of their Pakistani culture. Yasmin loves to share facts about Pakistan!

Location

Pakistan is on the continent of Asia, with India on one side and Afghanistan on the other.

Islamabad

PAKISTAN

Founder

Muhammad Ali Jinnah was the founder of Pakistan.

500

Heroes

Abdul Sattar Edhi was a Pakistani humanitarian who created the world's largest volunteer ambulance network. He is considered a Pakistani hero.

Two people have won the Nobel Prize from Pakistan: Malala Yousafzai for Peace in 2014 and Abdus Salam for Physics in 1979.

Make a Paper Bag Superhero!

SUPPLIES:

- lunch-size paper bag
- construction paper
- scissors
- markers or crayons
- glue stick or tape
- pipe cleaners
- optional: glitter, yarn (for hair),
  other art supplies

STEPS:

1. Flatten the paper bag and put bottom of bag at top. Draw eyes and a mouth on the folded part of the bag.

2. Cut a mask out of construction paper, or draw one on with marker. Use construction paper to make a cape. Decorate the mask and cape however you like! Glue them onto the paper bag to make the superhero's costume.

3. Glue or tape pipe cleaners to the sides of the bag for the superhero's arms.

4. Create a logo for the front of your superhero. Use your initial or draw a symbol. Use other art supplies to add finishing touches to your superhero, and you're done!

About the Author

Saadia Faruqi is a Pakistani American writer, interfaith activist, and cultural sensitivity trainer previously profiled in *O Magazine*. She is author of the adult short story collection, *Brick Walls: Tales of Hope & Courage from Pakistan*. Her essays have been published in *Huffington Post*, *Upworthy*, and *NBC Asian America*. She resides in Houston, Texas, with her husband and children.

About the Illustrator

Hatem Aly is an Egyptian-born illustrator whose work has been featured in multiple publications worldwide. He currently lives in beautiful New Brunswick, Canada, with his wife, son, and more pets than people. When he is not dipping cookies in a cup of tea or staring at blank pieces of paper, he is usually drawing books. One of the books he illustrated is *The Inquisitor's Tale* by Adam Gidwitz, which won a Newbery Honor and other awards, despite Hatem's drawings of a farting dragon, a two-headed cat, and stinky cheese.

Join Yasmin
on all her adventures!

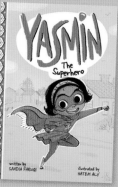

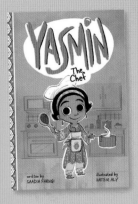

Discover more at
www.capstonekids.com